HANS IN LUCK

Retold from Grimm and with pictures
by

David McKee

Abelard-Schuman
London New York Toronto

Once upon a time there was a young man called Hans. For seven years he worked with one master.

One morning Hans said to his master, "I should like to go home to see my mother. Will you give me my wages, please, and allow me to go?"

"Certainly Hans," said his master. "You have worked hard, and I shall reward you well." And he gave Hans a lump of silver the size of his head. Hans wrapped it in a huge spotted handkerchief, rested it upon his shoulder and, waving good-bye to his master, left for home.

Hans gradually walked slower and slower as his load seemed to get heavier and heavier. A gentleman on a horse came along, and Hans, full of envy, said, "How lucky you are just to sit and be taken quickly wherever you want to go. My load is silver, but it is a burden which is slowing my journey home to my mother."

"To help you reach your mother," smiled the gentleman, "I will exchange my horse for your silver."

Delighted with the exchange, Hans was soon riding off. "If you want to go faster just shout 'Jip'," the gentleman called after him.

Soon Hans was quite used to the horse's speed. Then, thinking it would be nice to go faster and get home sooner, he shouted "Jip!"

The horse jumped forward with a rush. Taken by surprise, Hans was thrown out of the saddle and into a ditch beside the road.

A farmer, who happened to be passing with a cow, managed to catch the horse. Hans, feeling miserable, clambered to his feet. "What a brute," he said. "He's useless, not like your docile cow. You can walk along safely at your own speed, and have milk to drink and butter and cheese to eat whenever you like."

"Since you are so unhappy with your horse," said the farmer, "if you like I will exchange my cow for him." At once Hans was smiling again and the bargain was made. With a wave of his hand, the farmer rode away on the horse, leaving Hans to lead the cow.

Hans walked on, leading the cow, until he came to an inn where he stopped and rested. He spent his last money on food and drink, and went on his way refreshed. "When I get thirsty again I shall milk the cow," he said to himself.

As the day went by the sun became hotter, and as the sun became hotter, Hans became thirstier. When his thirst became unbearable Hans decided it was time to milk the cow. Using his hat as a bucket, he sat down on a stone. No sooner did he try to milk the cow than she gave a start and, throwing up her legs, kicked Hans unconscious.

Fortunately, a man came along wheeling a barrow with a pig in it. He gave Hans a drink from his flask and, after reviving him, said, "You will never milk that old cow! She is fit only for the slaughterhouse."

Hans sighed, "I never enjoy beef. If only I could have a pig such as yours, I would be happy."

"Well," the man said, "you take the pig and I'll take the cow."

Hans quickly agreed and they parted, each taking the other's animal.

Shortly after, Hans met a man with a goose and stopped to speak to him. "Look at my fine pig," said Hans. "Have you ever seen a better one?"

"It is a fine animal," said the other, "but I am glad I am not taking it into the next town. A pig which looks just like this one has been stolen. The owner will kill the thief if he catches him."

"What can I do?" moaned Hans.

"Well, I could help you by taking the pig, because I am going away from the town," replied the man. "You could have the goose in exchange. I think I ought to have something else as well, but since you have nothing else, I will not refuse to help you."

Gratefully, Hans made the exchange right away.

Hans walked on to the town, saying to himself, "While the goose is alive, I shall have eggs. When I kill her, she will make me a fine meal, and her feathers will fill a pillow."

He was pleased with the latest exchange.

In the town Hans met a tinker who was sharpening knives.

"Where did you get that fine goose?" asked the tinker.

"I exchanged a pig for it," answered Hans.

"And how did you get the pig?" he was asked.

"In exchange for a cow."

"And the cow?"

"In exchange for a horse," Hans replied.

"And how did you get the horse?"

"In exchange for a lump of silver the size of my head."

"And where did you get the silver?" went on the tinker.

"I worked seven hard years for that," said Hans.

"What you want," said the tinker, "is work like mine. A tinker always has money in his pocket."

"That would indeed be wonderful," said Hans.

"Now here," continued the tinker, "is a stone which is rough, but with a little working would sharpen a rusty nail to a razor's edge. You can have it in exchange for the goose." And the tinker picked up from beside the road an ordinary stone about the size of Hans's head.

Hans was delighted and, handing over the goose, he wrapped the stone in his huge spotted handkerchief. Then he put it on his shoulder and walked on his way.

Hans continued on his journey. He passed through the town and finally left it. Gradually, he walked slower and slower as his load seemed to get heavier and heavier. Soon he became thirsty again and looked forward to finding a place where he would be able to get a drink.

When he reached a fresh-looking pool, Hans put down his stone and wiped his brow with the spotted handkerchief. Then, kneeling down to drink from the pool, he bumped the stone. It fell into the pool with a *plop* and sank to the bottom.

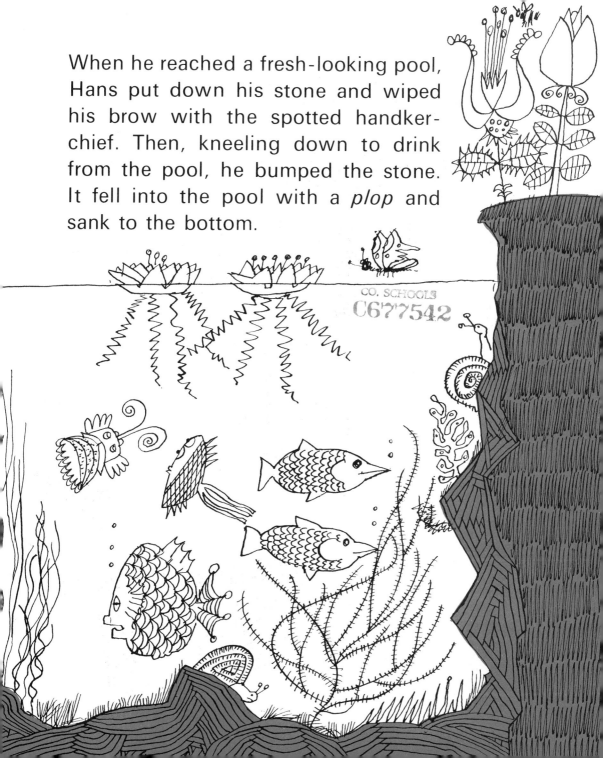

Hans stared down at the stone, then finished his drink.

Well, thought Hans, I have had many lucky exchanges but this is the greatest piece of luck I have had. Now I have no burden and nothing to worry about.

Then, full of happiness, he finished his journey home to his mother.